First Facts™

Simple Machines to the Rescue

Screws
to the Rescue

by Sharon Thales

Consultant:
Louis A. Bloomfield, PhD
Professor of Physics
University of Virginia
Charlottesville, Virginia

WITHDRAWN

Fitchburg Public Library
5530 Lacy Road
Fitchburg, WI 53711

Capstone
press®
Mankato, Minnesota

First Facts is published by Capstone Press,
151 Good Counsel Drive, P.O. Box 669, Mankato, Minnesota 56002.
www.capstonepress.com

Copyright © 2007 by Capstone Press. All rights reserved.
No part of this publication may be reproduced in whole or in part, or stored in a retrieval system,
or transmitted in any form or by any means, electronic, mechanical, photocopying, recording, or
otherwise, without written permission of the publisher.
For information regarding permission, write to Capstone Press,
151 Good Counsel Drive, P.O. Box 669, Dept. R, Mankato, Minnesota 56002.
Printed in the United States of America, North Mankato, Minnesota.

Library of Congress Cataloging-in-Publication Data
Thales, Sharon.
    Screws to the rescue / Sharon Thales.
    p. cm.—(First facts. Simple machines to the rescue)
    Summary: "Describes screws, including what they are, how they work, past uses, and
common uses of these simple machines today"—Provided by publisher.
    Includes bibliographical references and index.
    ISBN-13: 978-0-7368-6749-8 (hardcover)
    ISBN-10: 0-7368-6749-X (hardcover)
    1. Screws—Juvenile literature. I. Title. II. Series.
TJ1338.T43 2007
621.8'82—dc22   2006021502

Editorial Credits
Becky Viaene, editor; Thomas Emery, designer; Kyle Grenz, illustrator; Jo Miller,
    photo researcher/photo editor

Photo Credits
Capstone Press/Karon Dubke, 5, 12 (both), 13 (both), 14–15, 18–19, 21 (all); TJ Thoraldson
    Digital Photography, cover
Corbis/Bettmann, 11; Koopman, 17
Getty Images Inc./Time Life Pictures/Mansell, 8
Shutterstock/Mikhail Kondrashov, 6

072010
5843VMI

Table of Contents

A Helpful Screw

You want to drink a soda in the van. If you open a soda can, it may spill everywhere.

Screw to the rescue!

Take a soda bottle instead. The bumpy ridge of the bottle top is a **screw**. It holds the bottle and cap together and keeps you from spilling.

Work It

A screw is a **simple machine**. Simple machines have one or no moving parts. Machines are used to make **work** easier.

Work is using a **force** to move an object. Screws usually do work by holding objects together. These simple machines have been helping people for thousands of years.

Screw Fact

Not sure what a screw looks like? Look at a spiral staircase. Like other screws, this staircase is an inclined plane wrapped around a post.

A Screw in Time

Ancient Egyptian farmers needed water from the Nile River to grow crops. How could they get water from the river up to their fields?

Screw to the rescue!

Farmers put one end of a tube into the water. Then they turned a large screw inside the tube. The screw pushed water up the tube to the fields.

Screw Fact

The Egyptian water screw was called an "Archimedes screw." It was invented by a scientist named Archimedes.

Ancient Greeks and Romans used olive oil for many things from cooking to making soap. But they needed a better way to squeeze oil out of olives.

They made big wooden screw presses and put olives inside. When they turned the screws, two boards pressed together and oil came out of the olives.

screw press

11

What Would We Do Without Screws?

Do you want to talk on the phone or use the computer? Screws to the rescue! Screws hold items together so you can use them.

Screws

Screws hold together many items that you use every day. Some screws are very tiny. Can you find the screws on your video game system?

You can find screws outside too. Screws hold reflectors onto your bike. They also hold swing sets together and tree forts together.

Screw Fact

Screws can be wider than your arm is long! People use giant screws to drill holes in the earth.

Working Together

A pencil sharpener is a **complex machine.** It is made of several simple machines. The handle is a wheel that turns the axle and two screws. The threads on the screws are made of sharp wedges. The wedges scrape against a pencil to sharpen it.

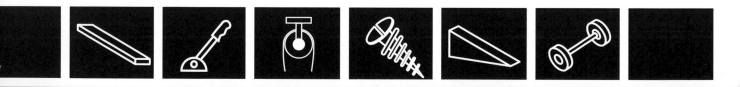

Screw Buddies

Six kinds of simple machines combine to make almost every machine there is.

- **Inclined plane**–a slanting surface that is used to move objects to different levels
- **Lever**–a bar that turns on a resting point and is used to lift items
- **Pulley**–a grooved wheel turned by a rope, belt, or chain that often moves heavy objects
- **Screw**–an inclined plane wrapped around a post that usually holds objects together
- **Wedge**–an inclined plane that moves to split things apart or push them together
- **Wheel and axle**–a wheel that turns around a bar to move objects

Screw

Wheel and Axle

Screws Everywhere

Most items have screws in them. Tiny screws hold eyeglasses and sunglasses together. The bumpy ridges on the bottom of light bulbs are also screws. They connect the bulbs to sockets to help give us light. Screws come to our rescue every day.

Tank

Screws

Blade

Screws can even make ice smooth for you to skate on. As the Zamboni machine moves across the rink, a blade shaves off a thin layer of ice. Inside the Zamboni, giant screws turn to pick up the ice and move it to the Zamboni's tank. Then the Zamboni spreads water on the rink to make a smooth new layer of ice.

Hands On: Working with a Screw

What You Need

3 inch (8 centimeter) long nail, bar of soap, screw (same size as nail)

What You Do

1. Push the nail into the bar of soap, as far as you can.
2. Twist the screw into the bar of soap, as far in as the nail.

Which was easier to get into the soap? Which one took longer? It was easier to twist the screw into the soap, but it also took longer. The work was spread over a longer distance.

Glossary

complex machine (KOM-pleks muh-SHEEN)—a machine made of two or more simple machines

force (FORSS)—a push or a pull

screw (SKROO)—an inclined plane wrapped around a post that usually holds objects together

simple machine (SIM-puhl muh-SHEEN)—a tool with one or no moving parts that moves an object when you push or pull; screws are simple machines.

work (WURK)—when a force moves an object

Read More

Dahl, Michael. *Twist, Dig, and Drill: A Book about Screws.* Amazing Science. Minneapolis: Picture Window Books, 2005.

Oxlade, Chris. *Screws.* Useful Machines. Chicago: Heinemann Library, 2003.

Tieck, Sarah. *Screws.* Simple Machines. Edina, Minn.: Abdo, 2006.

Internet Sites

FactHound offers a safe, fun way to find Internet sites related to this book. All of the sites on FactHound have been researched by our staff.

Here's how:

1. Visit *www.facthound.com*

2. Choose your grade level.

3. Type in this book ID **073686749X** for age-appropriate sites. You may also browse subjects by clicking on letters, or by clicking on pictures and words.

4. Click on the **Fetch It** button.

FactHound will fetch the best sites for you!

Index